I0621479

Final Rest

a Murder Mystery

by

Nathan Birr

Published by BEACON BOOKS

Cover Images Copyright ©
Paul Craft/Shutterstock.com

ISBN: 978-1-7374270-6-3

www.nathanbirr.com

Books by Nathan Birr

Follow the exploits of P.I. Jackson Douglas in the ten volumes of *The Douglas Files*:

Overnight Delivery
Three's a Crowd
All an Illusion
Shot List
Chasing the Wind

Blood and Treasure
One Life to Lose
Golden Key
Mine to Avenge
Nine Lives

Also check out four *Douglas Files* shorts:

Black Male
WinterKill

Short Sail
As Good As Dead

Take a journey (and have an adventure) in *The Last Resort* series:

Fire & Ice
Broken Trust

The Fountain
Backs Against the Wall

Independent Stories:

God, Girls, Golf & the Gridiron . . . Not Always in That Order (A Love Story)
The Book of Levi
All is Calm?
Augusta Whispers

Non-Fiction:

Rights or Wrong? Examining the Declaration of Independence in the Light of Scripture

www.nathanbirr.com

one

IT WASN'T A particularly grisly scene, as far as murders go. The deceased's body was reclined on a fainting couch beneath the window, her head resting on the arm of the couch at a natural angle. Her left arm was folded across the wrinkled fabric of a navy blue peplum pencil dress, the fingers slightly curled over her waist. Her right arm hung off the couch, as if reaching for the martini glass that had fallen and broken and spilled its contents on the floor. She wore matching blue pumps, her left foot hanging off the end of the couch, and her right grazing the floor with her knee bent at a forty-five-degree angle. It looked as if she had collapsed on the couch after a hard day's work and accidentally fallen asleep . . .

Except for the bullet hole in the middle of her forehead.

It didn't take a private detective like me to figure out what had killed her. Nor to determine she'd been murdered. For one thing, women don't blow their brains out; they're too vain to damage their faces. Women drink poison or swallow pills or jump off a bridge or swim out to sea. For another, nobody--women or men--blows their brains out and then disposes of the gun. And there was no gun.

The wound was small, the size of a .22 caliber bullet. A .22 isn't a particularly powerful weapon, but if fired from close range, it gets the job done. I know; I own a small .22 Smith & Wesson revolver. You can't be too careful in my line of work. Or in this neighborhood.

The scene wasn't completely sterile. There was the obvious blood splatter--a little on the couch, a little on the dress, a little on the victim's hair, which was a color somewhere between brown and gray. And there was blood on her face, which almost obscured a cut and a forming bruise on the left side of her head, beside her eye. It was a new cut, with a trail of fresh blood beneath it. Whoever had shot her had whacked her first.

The victim's name was Margaret Gorbachev, but everybody called her "Daisy." For as long as I've known, she's owned and run the Palisades Club. Word on the street is she used to sing, with a sultry, soulful voice that could practically command men right out of their seats. Rumor also had it she'd been so beautiful she could charm them into almost anything without uttering a word. Looking at Daisy now, she still had the frame of a beautiful woman, but the years had not been kind to a face that was rugged and hard, or to a voice that had become a rasping growl. That might have been attributed to years of smoking too.

After examining the body for a minute, I turned to Officer Sherman. He's the beat cop in the neighborhood, a pretty good one too, if not a little too straight-laced for my taste. But he does good work, and in a city where the cops are overworked and underpaid, I appreciate that. He's also not on the take, which is worth noting. He and I trust each other, which is why he calls me and why I answer when he does. Plus it was a slow night, and I never mind an excuse to visit the Palisades Club.

"Anybody been in here since you arrived?" I asked Sherman.

He shook his head. "Just you and me."

I nodded. I stepped back and looked around the room. Daisy's office was on the second floor of the club, across the hall from a dressing room and a break room. It wasn't a big office, much smaller than mine a few blocks over, and the window looked out on the side alley. It was slightly ajar, which allowed the hiss of a steady drizzle to waft in on the same breeze that stirred the drawn curtains. The walls were covered with posters and signed photographs of would-be and has-been stars, most of whom I didn't recognize. There was also some artwork, avant-garde stuff, junk I wouldn't let other people know I owned, much less display. I'd been in Daisy's office once before, and, as expected, it looked the same.

I walked around a desk on the far wall, pushed back the chair, and stood behind the desk. I lifted my head, looking at Daisy's body on the couch. Sherman stood at the door, his cap in his hand, as if paying respects. I examined the desk.

It was a mess. Papers everywhere. But they didn't get my attention first. A thin, opaque vase did. Or, more accurately, a bundle of two dozen dead daisies supported by the rim of the vase as they fell over it. A small card was tucked into the stems.

I pointed at the card. "You look at this?" I asked Sherman.

"I haven't touched a thing, TJ, except . . . Daisy, when I felt her pulse."

I should have known, a by the book cop wouldn't have contaminated the scene. I didn't have to worry about that anymore, so I plucked the card from the stems and flipped it over to read a short note that had been typewritten on it.

"Who's P?" I asked.

Sherman shrugged.

"You get what you deserve," I said, holding the card out. He approached and took it, then read it aloud himself.

"P," he said, as if musing. But he said nothing more. So I turned my attention to the other contents of the desk.

Sitting on top of the stack was a budget worksheet, going back several months. Quite a bit of red ink. That the Palisades Club was struggling was no secret. Daisy had kept it going by sheer willpower, I think. A quick survey of the worksheet gave no indication that Daisy was cooking the books, but I'm no accountant.

Beside the budget worksheet and partially tucked underneath it was a sheet of paper with a list of dates and corresponding numbers. Hours worked, if I had to guess, and I did. "Charlie" was scrawled on top. Charlie is the waitress downstairs. She isn't the only employee, but she is the only one whose hours were being tallied separately.

Half a dozen bar tabs were stuck on a bill spike at the front of the desk. None of the names looked familiar. None of the amounts were worth killing over, either, but then again, each man has his own price. People in this city had been killed for less, I'm sure. Positive, in fact. I've investigated the killings.

Beside the bill spike I found a letter from the bank. Daisy was behind a month's payment on the mortgage for the club. That went hand in hand with the red ink on the budget sheet. But no bank I knew of found it financially prudent to shoot borrowers with outstanding debts.

Near the corner of the desk, partially obscured by more papers, was an ashtray. I looked at the papers first, a copy of the Palisades Club's tax return. I was curious why it was sitting out, so I scanned it. Nothing jumped out at me, from a numbers perspective. But a name did. Joshua Palermo was listed as a part owner of the club. That was news to me.

Joshie "The Rat" Palermo is a small-time mobster with his hands in everything--

drugs and booze, money laundering, girls, bookmaking. The Rat is a real piece of slime, and like slime, he can get out of almost anything. The cops have never been able to make charges stick, and it wouldn't surprise me if one day they stop playing fair. I've even thought once or twice about taking the law into my own hands. The worst part is that The Rat interacts with regular people as if he's one of them, not a punk gangster. He's often at the Palisades Club, and now I knew why: he's invested.

I dropped the tax return back on the desk, beside the ashtray. It was empty but for a few ashes and one cigarette stub. It had been smoked only a quarter, and I could identify it as a Camel. I nodded at it, then at Sherman. "What brand did Daisy smoke?"

"Excuse me?"

"What brand of cigarette did Daisy smoke?"

"I don't know."

I rifled through the drawers of the desk, finding nothing of any interest. In the center drawer, I found two packs of Chesterfield cigarettes. I held one up. "Not Camels."

"The cigarette isn't Daisy's," Sherman declared.

I shook my head.

"The killer's, you think?"

"Unless she was entertaining tonight," I said before closing the drawer. I looked back to the desk, to see if I'd missed anything.

"Did you see the safe?" Sherman asked.

I looked at him, then to the left, to the square combination safe on the floor against the wall. The door was ajar, and the safe was empty. I looked back to Sherman. "Yeah, I saw the safe."

I stepped around the desk and squatted down, brushing aside the flap of my tan trench coat. I opened the safe door all the way, revealing it was in fact completely empty. Still crouched, I looked toward Daisy's body on the couch. A bullet hole in the forehead and a cut and bruise on the side of the head. "The killer brandished his gun," I said, holding my thumb and forefinger like a gun as I talked to myself and to Sherman. "He smacked her with it to show he meant business." I stood. "He forced her to open the safe, she stood back, and then he shot her and she fell back on the couch."

Sherman nodded. "Could be."

"Could be," I said. I looked carefully around one more time. Nothing else stood out. "You say Moose found her?"

"That's right."

"Where's he now?"

"Waiting at his post."

I nodded. Moose is the bouncer, for lack of better term, at the Palisades Club. Unless he was tossing out riffraff--and from time to time there was riffraff at the Palisades Club that needed to be tossed out--he hung out in a little alcove just offstage where he could see the performers, the bar, and most of the dining room. He could also see up the stairs, to the base of the dressing room door and the base of Daisy's office door. He could not see the door to the alley. But he might have seen something relevant.

"Would you go get him?" I asked.

Sherman nodded.

He left, and I lit a cigarette, then drew a handkerchief from my coat pocket. It was clean enough, and I draped it over Daisy's face. She deserved at least that much.

two

I TURNED AS I heard a shuffling of steps
and looked up to see Moose.

He got the name honest.

Moose is six-foot-six, and weighs at least
two-seventy or two-eighty. Maybe three bills,
I don't know. He's big. He was dressed, as
always, in black. His skin is also black, but
I'm not sure I can say it that way. We used
to call him "colored," but I think that's
wrong now too. I don't know the right way to
describe it, and I don't really care. I also
don't care what color a person's skin is, as

long as they're a decent person, and Moose is. He is a little clumsy, though. He can still do his job just fine, but maybe don't ask him to balance a tray on his shoulder like Charlie does. He's also a little slow mentally, but that may be reticence more than anything. After all, people who look like Moose aren't generally considered to have anything worth saying. I was about to test that.

"Mr. James," he said with a nod of his head. His voice was deep and yet had a childlike quality to it. Might be that reticence again.

"Moose," I said. "You found Daisy?"

He nodded his head.

"Tell me what happened," I said, then took a drag on my cigarette.

"Miss Lizzie was finishin' her song when I heard a loud bang. I come up the stairs and see somebody goin' out the back door there," he said, pointing down the hall, which he still stood in. "I knocked on Miss Daisy's door, and nobody answered. I knocked a second time, and then I opened the door. I was afraid somethin' had happened to her."

"And she was laying just like this?"

"Yes, sir, Mr. James. 'Cept she didn't have no handkerchief over her face."

Despite the circumstance, I couldn't help but crack a smile. "What'd you do next, Moose?"

"I called her name. 'Miss Daisy!' I yelled. 'Miss Daisy!' I saw the bullet hole, but I called her name anyhow." His lip trembled as he added, "She didn't answer me." Moose swallowed. "I remembered the man I saw, so I ran to the alley door. There wasn't nobody there. So I ran to the street and hollered. Officer Sherman was just across the street and came right away."

I nodded. "This man you saw leaving, you get a good look at him?"

"Not his face. Just his back as he ducked out."

"You see what he was wearing?"

Moose nodded. "A trench coat."

"A trench coat." I tugged the flap of my coat. "Like this one, or was it darker? Maybe black?"

Moose squinted. "Yeah. A black trench coat."

"He have a hat?" I asked.

"I don't remember."

"Hair color?"

"I don't remember. I'm sorry, Mr. James."

"That's okay, Moose. Was the person tall, short, was he big or small?"

"Everybody looks small compared to me."

I grinned again at Moose and puffed on the cigarette. "You remember anything else about him?"

"No."

"Okay. You did good, Moose."

His posture sagged a little.

I exhaled smoke. "This door usually unlocked?"

He nodded. "Miss Daisy didn't lock it when she was inside, unless she had a special reason to."

I frowned. Something about the way he said "Miss Daisy" bugged me, but I couldn't figure out what it was.

"What about the alley door?" I asked.

"That was always locked from the inside."

"Who has keys?"

"Miss Daisy, and all the staff."

"You?"

"Yes, Mr. James."

"Anybody else?"

Moose shook his head.

"You look at the door?" I asked Sherman, who'd stood beside Moose the whole time.

"It didn't look jimmied."

"So whoever killed her had a key," I said.

"Or came from inside."

"Past Moose?"

"Nobody came past me, Mr. James, I promise you that."

"They could have used the back stairway," Sherman said. In addition to the stairs that Moose could see from his alcove, a second set led up from beside the bar and entered the hallway between the dressing room and the break room. Somebody could have come up those stairs without Moose seeing them, and could maybe have gotten into Daisy's office if Moose had been looking away. But it would have been risky.

"When I arrived," he said, "after checking the scene and talking with Moose, I went downstairs and took some brief statements, just asking if anyone had seen anything. No one had. Before I called you, I called the station to have Officer O'Brien join me. We made sure nobody left until you had a chance to question them."

"Who all's here?"

"All the staff, a few of the Saturday night regulars. Moose said most people left after Lizzie was done."

"It was a small crowd tonight," Moose said.

"And they all know what happened?"

"Yes, sir, Mr. James."

"Is the Rat here?" I asked, thinking of the daisies and the tax return showing him as part owner.

"He's here," Sherman said, "along with a couple of his . . ."

"Goons," Moose said.

"Mr. Caldwell from the bank?" I asked.

"No, Mr. James."

"Charlie working tonight?"

"Every night."

I thought of the daisies again, signed with the single letter "P." I inhaled nicotine. "Peaches here?"

Sherman swallowed. "She is. You don't think . . ."

"Miss Daisy didn't much care for Peaches," Moose said.

"Neither do a lot of people," I added.

"Still, as a motive for murder?" Sherman said.

"People have killed for less." I looked back to Moose. "Like The Rat, maybe."

"Why would he kill Daisy?" Sherman asked.

I kept looking at Moose, hoping to prod him if he had something to contribute. And he did.

"Miss Daisy didn't much care for him either."

"Why's that?"

"Miss Daisy got herself into some financial trouble a few years back, and Mr. Palermo bailed her out . . . for a price."

"What price?" Sherman asked when I didn't.

"She made him a part owner of the club."

I puffed on the cigarette again. Moose looked like he wanted to say more, and I took a step closer. "There something else?"

"A couple months ago, Mr. Palermo tried to buy out Miss Lizzie's contract. But Miss Daisy wasn't havin' none of that. She told me he even tried to lure Miss Lizzie away, to just leave and come work for him. Offered her big money, said not to worry about Miss Daisy. When Miss Daisy found out, she got real mad. Miss Lizzie said Miss Daisy hit Mr. Palermo on the head with an old baseball bat."

"Probably broke the bat on that head," I said.

"Yes, sir, Mr. James," Moose said with a chuckle. "That's a good one, Mr. James."

I took another drag on the cigarette. Lizzie was the main attraction at the Palisades Club. To call her pretty would be insulting, just like saying she had a divine voice would be. When she was on stage, pouring her soul into that microphone, everything else in the room faded away. The thought of her being affiliated with somebody like The Rat--never mind what sort of work he would have lured her to--was enough to turn a guy's stomach.

"Mr. James?"

I blinked and turned to Moose. "Yeah?"

"There is something else I just thought of. About Miss Lizzie, I mean."

"What's that?"

"I saw her talkin' to somebody this evening, before the show."

"Who was it?"

"I don't know. See, she was standin' by the stage door, and whoever she was talkin' to was outside. It wasn't none of my business, so I let her have privacy."

"Good policy, Moose."

He nodded. "I just know after that, she seemed happier."

"Happier?"

"She seemed awful sad today."

"Sad?"

"Not like cryin' or nothin', but she just wasn't her normal self, wasn't happy like Miss Lizzie usually is. Been that way a couple of days now. But after that, she was smilin' again and winked at me and said 'Hi, Moose' all cheerful like right before she went on stage."

I nodded. "No idea who she was talking to?"

"No, sir."

"Okay."

"I sure do respect Miss Lizzie," Moose said. "Especially the way Miss Daisy treats . . . I mean, the way she treated her."

"What do you mean?" Sherman asked, having been silent for several minutes. I shot him a glance, then looked at Moose.

"It's no secret Miss Daisy was hard on Miss Lizzie. Wouldn't let her out of her contract, not for Mr. Palermo and not when Miss Lizzie asked."

"Lizzie wanted out of her contract?"

"For a long time, Officer Sherman. She felt it wasn't fair, Miss Daisy makin' all that money from her singin'."

"Daisy gave her a place to sing, didn't she?"

"Sure did. And paid her. But Miss Lizzie thought Miss Daisy could have been fairer with her, and with everybody."

"She tell you this?" Sherman asked.

Moose nodded. Then slowly morphed to shaking his head. "She'd yell at her too, Miss Daisy would, over little things. Not singin' a certain song on a certain night, or singin' too long. The way she dressed, sometimes, all sorts of stuff. I even saw her hit Miss Lizzie once, slapped her right across the face for askin' for a night off. She was too hard on her, and I even told her that once. She told me to mind my own business." Moose shrugged. "So I did."

I swallowed. I'd heard rumors that Daisy had been a hard mistress, and Lizzie bore the brunt of it. Then again, if you were an old battle axe whose beauty had faded and whose voice had turned to gravel, how would you feel about a glamorous starlet with a voice of honey stealing the spotlight?

"You don't think Miss Lizzie would . . . ?" Moose asked.

I shook my head. "Like you said, she was on stage when you heard the gunshot."

"Yeah, that's right."

I nodded toward Sherman. "Let's take a look at that door."

Moose stepped aside, and I followed Sherman to the alley door. It was a standard wood door, with a lock and a deadbolt. I looked at Moose. "The deadbolt ever used?"

"No, sir, Mr. James. Not that I've ever seen."

"Hmm." I opened the door, and was greeted by the tink, tink, tink of raindrops falling on the metal fire escape that led to the alley below. I took a step onto the fire escape, and the rain now made tat, tat, tat sounds on the brim of my hat and the shoulders of my coat. Both were still damp from my arrival a few minutes ago, when Sherman had let me in through the same door. Like before, the alley was black, lined by two- and three-story buildings on either side, with the only light coming from windows or the street. If a man in a black trench coat ran down the alley now, I'm not sure we'd have seen him. Or a woman in a black trench coat, for that matter.

The night was cool, and the rain more so, and there was nothing to see in the alley anyhow. Come daylight, Sherman and O'Brien could look for a gun, but I doubt they'd find one. Not the right one, anyhow.

"You want to interview people?" Sherman asked.

I flicked my cigarette butt into the night. Then I nodded and stepped back inside, and Sherman closed the door.

"Start with The Rat?"

I thought of the daisies again, of the tax return, of the Camel cigarette butt--a brand I was pretty sure from previous interactions with him that The Rat smoked. I thought that with a little luck, we might be able to pin this on him quick-like, and I could get back to my apartment before the whole night was gone. After all, I had a glass of cognac just waiting to be poured.

three

WE MADE IT halfway down the hall, me in front of Sherman and him a few steps in front of Moose, before plans changed. That's when I saw a golden swirl appear from the stairs, followed by an angelic face, and then the body of a goddess.

Her actual name is Elizabeth Gerald, but everybody I know calls her Lizzie. She wore a bright red dress--fire engine red, and it made sirens go off. It wasn't a sleazy dress; some of these girls at clubs like the Palisades Club wear sleazy dresses, and usually the dress fits the girl. Lizzie doesn't hide that she's a woman--she couldn't hide it--but she's classy. She doesn't prostitute herself to the audience, doesn't seduce them with some physical routine; she charms and teases in a good-natured way. Her music isn't bawdy or sensual, but powerful and stirring.

Back to that dress. Something in the material gave off a silvery shine, a sparkle, and long silver gloves--long as in to the elbow--brought out the sparkle even more, as did a pair of large hoop earrings. Her long, blond hair is usually styled up, sometimes with a few loose curls dangling beside her face. Tonight there were curls. And eyes blue as the bay on a sunny afternoon seem always to be looking at you--no, through you, to your very soul. Lizzie is worth the price of admission before she ever sings a note.

She crested the stairs and we all stopped. Lizzie strode toward us in stiletto heels that had to hurt the floor. I watched the slit in her dress as her lower leg pushed through it, then receded behind it, then pushed through it . . . I lifted my eyes to hers as she approached, stopping just in front of me.

"Oh, Mr. James, thank goodness you've come," she said, and threw herself into my arms. I caught her and held her--without complaint, mind you--while she sobbed on my shoulder. She was warm, whereas the night was cold, and I wouldn't have minded if she'd cried a little longer. But she stopped after just a moment and lifted her head to look at me. "You will catch whoever did this, won't you, Mr. James? You'll find them?"

"Of course I will, angel. Don't you worry about it."

She smiled, and I swear the rain outside stopped. "It's so horrible," she said, taking a step back, and seemingly noticing Sherman and Moose for the first time. "I just can't believe somebody would kill Daisy, right here in her own office."

"You mean as opposed to killing her somewhere else?" Sherman asked.

Lizzie cut her baby blues to Sherman. "No, of course not. I mean anywhere. It just seems more awful here."

"Did you hear anything?" I asked. "While you were singing, I mean?"

"No. I was focused on my song," she said, looking briefly at her hands. "I didn't . . . I didn't know until Moose told us."

"You know why anybody would want Daisy dead?"

"I won't lie. Daisy was a hard woman to work for. Not initially, but as time went on she seemed to grow jealous. I think she was bitter about life, about the weight she'd put on, about her voice. And she treated everyone harshly--me, Charlie, Al, even Moose." She shook her head. "But I just can't fathom someone killing her for it."

"I'll find whoever did it, Lizzie. Count on it."

She sagged her shoulders and smiled again, and I wished there was more I could promise her. Instead, I asked her to hang around, in case I had any more questions. She agreed, and I started past her down the hall. I stopped.

"Something wrong?" she asked.

I lifted my hand to gently tilt her head to the side. The hallway lighting wasn't great, and she wore enough makeup that I almost couldn't see the bruise on the left side of her face, just below and beside her eye.

"Daisy?" I asked.

Lizzie closed her eyes, looked down, and nodded.

So did I. Somebody was going to pay for what happened to Daisy, but I took satisfaction in knowing that Daisy was also paying for what she'd done.

four

LIZZIE SAID SHE was going to clear her head in the employee break room, and the three of us headed for the stairs she'd come up a few minutes earlier. At the top of them, Sherman reached out a hand to stop me. He looked back to where Lizzie had ducked into the break room, then said, "TJ, she has an awfully good motive."

"And an awfully good alibi," I said. "She was singing when Mocse heard the shot."

Sherman sighed. "Yeah."

"Besides, sounds like a lot of people had a motive for wanting Daisy dead, or at least for being angry with her."

He conceded with a nod, and we went downstairs. At the base of the stairs, we could have gone left to an alcove stage left where a performer could wait to go on or someone could watch them while hidden from the audience. Instead, we walked behind a large polyester curtain that served as the backdrop for the stage. Bypassing several storage closets, we stopped at the back corner of the stage, and also the back corner of the building. This was an alcove similar to the one on the other side, only with an unobstructed view of the dining room and the bar. It also had a view, behind the backdrop curtain, of the stairs and the base of them on the second level. A sturdy stool in the corner marked Moose's usual location during a performance.

I looked out at the dining room, at occupants scattered around a dozen tables. I recognized a few of them, including Peaches and The Rat.

I turned to Moose. "You were on this stool when you heard the shot?"

"Yes, sir, Mr. James."

I pursed my lips. Maybe he'd heard it because he was trained to hear unusual things, to pay attention to something other than the act on stage. Or maybe he'd heard it because the sound traveled down behind the curtain, in a straight line. Or maybe he'd heard it because it was a gunshot, and gunshots are loud, and somebody else had heard it too. Then again, that Daisy had been shot in the head wasn't in question. And while it would be good to have a corroborating witness as to the time of the gunshot, I didn't question Moose's report.

I scanned the dining room again. There were two patrons still at the bar, guys, and I didn't recognize either of them. There were couples at three tables, one I recognized, one I didn't, and one I couldn't place. Eight people, none of whom were suspects. Any of them *might* have had a motive for wanting Daisy dead, but I decided to concentrate on more likely culprits.

The Rat and his two "goons" were at a table in the corner, in the darkness, where they belonged. Peaches sat at a table by herself in the center of the room, almost as if the spotlight belonged on her. Al was behind the bar, and Charlie was, like always, working, making sure all these sequestered guests were taken care of. I wondered if the realization that her employer was dead had even hit her.

I decided to let my prime suspects marinate for a few minutes, and turned my eyes across the relatively small stage to a baby grand piano. It was sleek and black, shining under the spotlights. The man behind it was old, pushing eighty if he was a day, and it showed in a slightly stooped back and receding hair that was gray where it wasn't white. He had a mustache, a thinnish one, and moved slowly as if every movement caused him pain. The exception was when his hands flew across the keys of that baby grand. He'd accompanied Lizzie and every other performer at the Palisades Club for years--decades, in fact--and still tickled those ivories as he had in his youth, presumably. I'd never learned his real name, because it didn't matter. He was affectionately known by everyone as "Gramps." Even crusty, old Daisy had a soft spot in her heart for him.

"Go ahead and take a load off," I said to Moose, then nodded for Sherman to follow me. I was sure the folks scattered around the dining room saw me, and I walked slowly to make sure they did. I wanted them squirming.

"Evening, Gramps," I said, leaning against the edge of the piano.

"Evening, Mr. James," he said with a thin grin and a nod. "Officer Sherman," he said with another nod.

"Go ahead and keep playing," I said, in part because the soft melody he was coaxing one-handed from the piano was soothing, and in part because sound carried, and I wanted to be sure our conversation was private.

"You got a request?" he asked.

"I do," I said, eying the glass jar for tips on the end of the piano. "But I'm tapped."

"Oh, it's no charge to you, Mr. James."

"I like that French tune, 'La Mer.' You know it?"

"Sure I know it, sonny." He began playing and, even with a dead body upstairs, it brought a smile to my face.

"You were playing for Lizzie tonight?" I asked.

Gramps nodded. "Always."

"Did you hear the gunshot?"

"Nope. I was into the performance. She did a wonderful job tonight, Lizzie. Then again . . ." he played the last few notes of the verse. "She always does."

"How was your relationship with Daisy?"

"Oh, Daisy and I go way back. She's got her rough edges, to be true, but who among us doesn't?"

"Did you know about how she treated Lizzie?" Sherman asked.

"Like I said, she had rough edges."

"Did Daisy hit Lizzie?"

Gramps looked at him. "If she did, I never saw it. I never saw her hit anyone."

"Not even The Rat?" I asked.

That made Gramps grin. "No, but I heard about that one." He played a few notes with a flourish. "If you're looking for motives, I won't deny Lizzie had one--a lot of people did, if they were the kind given to murder, I guess. Me too. Lizzie's like a granddaughter to me, and like I said, Daisy had rough edges, and she was harder on Lizzie and some of the others--Charlie, for example--than she needed to be. But," he said, finishing and turning to look directly at Sherman, then directly at me as he continued speaking, "I know Lizzie didn't do it because she was bringing the house down. The whole audience can vouch for her, and for me."

"We're just asking the questions we have to ask," I said. "I don't think Lizzie did it any more than I think you did."

He nodded and resumed tinkling on the piano, an indistinct tune this time.

"Was Daisy hard on you?" Sherman asked.

Gramps looked at him.

"You said she was hard on some of the others. Were you one of the some?"

"No."

"Why not?"

"Like I said, we go way back. I knew Daisy when she was . . . well, like Miss Lizzie."

"Young?" I asked.

"Successful?" Sherman asked.

"Beautiful," I said.

Gramps nodded again. "All of the above." He smiled to the music for a moment. "But, I don't want you to get the wrong idea about Daisy, either. The years hardened her, made her bitter in some ways, and she had those rough edges. But she was a strong woman, and it took everything she had to keep this place running, to keep people employed, to ward off the vultures circling," he said, casting a glance out into the dining room for the first time.

"Which vultures?" I asked.

"Joshie 'The Rat,' for one. Peaches."

"Peaches?" Sherman asked.

"She's been trying to buy this place for a while now. Made several offers, attractive ones. And Daisy could have used the money. But she didn't like Peaches, didn't like the disdain, didn't like the idea of Peaches transforming this club into something else. It may not be fancy, but it has substance; it appeals to regular people."

"And Peaches' vision didn't?"

"Peaches walks around as if regular people don't exist," Gramps said. "Maybe in her world they don't."

Sherman frowned.

"What about The Rat?" I asked.

"He's a minority owner, and from what Daisy let on, doing everything he could to squeeze her out and become a majority owner, if not sole owner."

"Everything he could? Like murder?"

Gramps played a few notes. "Daisy's dead, isn't she?"

"Did you see if The Rat was in his seat for the last song?" I asked.

"No, I didn't. When I'm playing, and when Lizzie's into a song, the room becomes a blur. I wish I could tell you I saw him get up just before she hit the finale and slip out of the room, but I can't." He shook his head. "Then again . . ." He paused to plunk a few notes. "I can't tell you he didn't either."

five

THE RAT DIDN'T get his nickname from his looks, but he could have. Round little eyes are sunken into his head, as if to make room for a long, pointed nose. His hair is dark, slicked back with so much gunk it looks like it's about to drip all over. The Rat is small with hunched little shoulders and a chin that disappears into his neck. He looks less like a mobster and more like the proverbial lackey a mobster smacks around.

But his appearance belies his reputation. Nobody messes with The Rat, and there are rumors he has friends in high places, an ability to manipulate things to his favor, things like criminal charges. He was flanked--figuratively and literally--by a couple of meatheads named Johnny-Boy and Tony-Boy. They're brothers, and I've never heard them talk. They don't need to. Where The Rat fails in physical intimidation, they more than make up for it. Word on the street is they aren't afraid even to muss up a beat cop or a private eye now and again. I had to tread carefully, and yet push The Rat's buttons. Like I said, there's a reason I carry a .22 revolver.

They sat at a round table, The Rat facing the stage with his back to the wall, the meatheads on either side of him. They wore cheap suits, gray, Johnny-Boy with his hair slicked back like his boss and Tony-Boy wearing a fedora with the front brim turned up, as if that made him tough. (It might have been Tony-Boy with the slicked hair and Johnny-Boy with the tough-brimmed hat, but I didn't care to distinguish between them.) The Rat's suit was cheap too, but a double-breasted deal that supposedly gave him some measure of prestige. His fedora, without the brim snapped up, sat on the table next to several empty glasses. Another glass, not empty, was at arm's reach.

He smirked at me as I approached. "Hello, Detective James."

I wanted to slap the smirk right off. But me smacking The Rat and the meatheads smacking me and Sherman and Officer O'Brien and probably Moose smacking them wouldn't get us anywhere. So I said, "Hello, Palermo."

"That's Mr. Palermo to you, crum," Johnny-Boy (I was pretty sure he was the slick-haired one) wheezed from Palermo's right. I was both amazed that he spoke and tempted to slap the stupid right off his face, but I couldn't swing hard enough for that. So I ignored him.

"Sit down," The Rat said, nodding at an empty chair at the table.

I ignored it too.

"I think you killed Daisy," I said, loud enough that others in the room could hear.

"I think you're full of crap," he answered me.

"That's not a denial."

He smirked again. "Why would I want to kill Daisy?"

"Knowing you, Palermo, for sport. Or maybe because you wanted a little bit more of the action at the club."

The smirk wavered for a second.

"Yeah, I know you're a part owner. How big a part, Palermo?"

"That's none of your business, Detective."

"It is if it pertains to Daisy's death," Sherman said from beside me.

"I ain't a-talking to you, copper."

"Maybe you'd like the copper to drag you by the collar of your cheap suit down to the station and ask you these questions there," I said.

The Rat stared at me, but said nothing.

"You put a bullet in Daisy's head, suddenly you're the only owner left. Figure you can, what, turn this place into a seedy little joint for you to run your operations out of, maybe smoke it up, hire some floozies to draw in the riffraff."

The smirk widened, and I was sorely tempted to knock it off, hang the consequences. But I exercised restraint.

"Thing of it is, Detective, Daisy was paranoid. Our contract stipulates that if she were to die, I'm out on my rear. I get nothing. It was her . . . insurance against just the sort of thing you're accusing me of."

I was taken aback, both by the revelation that Daisy had guarded against The Rat killing her, meaning he had no motive, and by the fact that he could properly use the word "stipulates" in a sentence.

"That's why I was trying to lure Lizzie away," The Rat said, leaning forward. "If I could take away Daisy's best act, cut down her profits, she might be inclined to get out of the club business and leave it all to me." He smirked again. "That and Lizzie's a real red-hot mama. Shame to be wasting her talents on just singing."

I stepped toward The Rat. Forget smacking the smirk off his face, I was going to squeeze his neck until that entire little head popped off and rolled across the floor. Tony-Boy stuck out a hand to stop me, and Sherman grabbed my arm from behind.

The Rat actually laughed. "I say something you disagree with, Detective? Or what, maybe you're jealous?"

"Yeah, I'm green with envy over a guy who hangs out with a couple of bums all day and has to pay his women."

That knocked the smirk off his face. "Why don't you go talk to one of these other guests, Detective, one of them who actually has a motive for killing Daisy?"

"Because I don't think you're as smart as you want me to think, Palermo. I think you're the kind to lose your cool, stop making good business decisions, and act on impulse. I still think you shot Daisy--maybe to get the club, maybe because you didn't like her terms, maybe because she once cracked you over your hard head with a ball bat, or maybe because you're a piece of garbage--and now you're trying to cover with some story about a contract. But I don't buy it for a second!"

He sat back and licked what little there was of his lips. "I'm the one who supposedly lost my cool, and you're the one foaming all over his chin."

I really wanted to belt him. The meatheads might do a number on me, but it'd almost be worth it.

The Rat had drawn a cigarette, and it was my chance to smirk. "Wouldn't happen to be a Camel, would it, Palermo?" I asked as he flicked a lighter at it.

He set down the lighter and drew the unlit cigarette from his mouth. "Why do you ask that?"

"Because we found the butt of a Camel in Daisy's ashtray, and she doesn't smoke Camels."

The Rat gave me a stony look, then reached into his suit pocket. I tensed until he withdrew a half-empty carton of cigarettes. He held the carton up for a second, then tossed it on the table. Even upside down, I could read the label: Lucky Strike.

"I switched," he said. "About a week ago."

I swallowed.

He lit his cigarette and took a long slow drag, exhaling a bluish puff of smoke into the air. "Want to see my piece, too, Detective? Wanna count the slugs? Wanna sniff the barrel?" He leaned forward, lifted the cigarette again, but spoke before taking a puff. "Or talk to some of the other guests, like I said, and they'll tell you I sat right here through Lizzie's entire routine." Now he puffed, then exhaled. "I wouldn't miss one second of that woman."

"So maybe you didn't pull the trigger yourself. You could have sat right here drooling and dreaming and had somebody else pop Daisy."

"I would too, hypothetically," he said, leaning on his elbow. The one holding the cigarette, and he took another hit. "But I would have had Johnny-Boy or Tony-Boy pull the trigger--hypothetically--and they were sitting here for the whole performance too." He sat back with that insidious smile again. "They're almost as big of Lizzie fans as I am, Detective. And maybe as you are?"

I was licked and I knew it. I went through the routine of having them all put their guns on the table, which they did. None were missing a round, none had been fired. That wasn't a surprise. I waited a minute, hoping against hope to think of something else I could use to trap The Rat. But I had nothing. I knew it, and he knew it.

So I told him not to leave just yet--I still had a little control--and turned for the bar. I wasn't going to make it home to that cognac anytime soon, and I was starting to really need a drink.

SIX

THE BAR AT the Palisades Club seats ten
or twelve people, in theory, but lacks a view
of the stage, which means it's empty when
people like Lizzie are on. Instead of watching
the stage, patrons at the bar stare at a
collage of old silent-film movie posters,
hideous wallpaper behind them, or a big
mirror straight out of a John Ford movie
saloon. Or they stare at the bartender, Al.
That would be my choice.

Al is actually Allison or Alice or
something like that, but everybody calls her

Al. Some of the less gentlemanly types call her plenty of other things, which is probably part of the reason she keeps her dark hair short--like a man might wear it, only choppier and sort of layered--and also dresses like a man--collared shirt, sometimes a tie, usually a vest. It's a classy look, but doesn't hide that she's a woman. Nor does the fact that she flirts shamelessly with male patrons, which likely elicits some of those comments and starts the cycle all over. Whatever, it's her life.

"Hey, James," she said as I approached. The two other patrons at the bar were nursing drinks, one in his own world and likely drunk, the other trying to act like he wasn't paying attention.

"Al," I said with a nod. "The usual please."

"Coming right up," she said with a wink, and turned to a bottle of Scotch--Johnny Walker Black, to be precise--on the back counter. She poured a couple fingers into a tumbler, then turned and set it on the counter in front of me. She held the bottle in the other hand. "Gonna need the bottle tonight?"

"We'll see," I said. I took a drink and let the smoky liquid burn my throat. "What do you know about who might have killed Daisy?"

"I know she wasn't real popular with most people."

"With you?" I asked, and took another drink.

Al shrugged. "Daisy was a tough boss. Made us work long hours, didn't pay us great. At least not me. But Pops sustained a family through the Depression, so I'm not going to complain."

"Anybody in particular seem to have a beef with her?"

"Lizzie seemed down lately. I know she feels stuck here."

I nodded. I reached for a cigarette. "You see anything unusual tonight?" I asked.

"I see unusual every night." Her eyes followed my lighter up to the cigarette, then watched me smoke. "Gosh, I could use one of those, but I'm out."

I smirked and set my pack of Old Gold on the counter.

"Not my brand," she said.

"And what is your brand?" I asked.

"Camels. Only person around here I know who smokes them is The Rat, and I'd rather lick out an ashtray than bum one off him."

I nodded and had a puff. "There was a Camel butt in Daisy's ashtray," I said.

"You ask The Rat about it?"

I nodded. "He seems to have an alibi."

She leaned forward, elbows on the counter. She was not wearing a vest, so her tie hung away from her shirt. It was black, with silver stripes, a sharp-looking deal. Why was I staring at her tie, as if that pattern or those colors meant something?

"You think I did it?"

That drew my eyes up to hers. I exhaled a puff of smoke. "Did you?"

"Yep. Right before Lizzie was finished, meaning right before everybody got up to get another drink, I stole up to Daisy's room, smoked my last cigarette, and shot her with a gun I don't have and then . . . left it there?

Threw it into the alley? Tucked it away somewhere?" She smirked. "Want to search behind the bar? Want to frisk me, James?"

"Yeah, but that's beside the point."

Her smirk got wider. Then she stood up and her tie straightened out. "The Rat have a *good* alibi?"

"Good enough."

"Check it carefully."

"Why do you say that? Because he's The Rat?"

"That, and I saw him arguing with Charlie earlier."

"Tonight?"

Al nodded. "Looked like it might get physical."

"Charlie's not the one dead."

"No, but something's got The Rat's tail. Tried to lure Lizzie away, tried to buy her away, now he's fighting with Charlie . . ."

"Any idea about what?"

"No."

"You said it looked like it might get physical?"

"He grabbed her arm. Looked like he was threatening her."

"Sounds like it did get physical."

Al shrugged.

I took a last drag on my cigarette and stamped it out in an ashtray. Then I downed the last of my Scotch. I reached for my wallet.

"It's on your tab, James."

"Thanks, kid."

"I hope you nail whoever did this," she said. "Daisy was a tough old bag, but I kind of liked her."

I nodded, took a moment to compose myself, and headed back to The Rat's table for round two.

seven

THIS TIME, THE Rat did not offer me a

seat. I took one anyhow, and ignored the glares from Johnny-Boy and Tony-Boy. I slowly lit another cigarette--they help me with stress--and promised myself I would play it cool this time.

"You must like my company," The Rat said after a minute of silence.

I made a point of slowly inhaling nicotine, then blowing it out in Johnny-Boy's general direction. I rotated my head around to The Rat.

"Tell me about Charlie."

"What's to tell?"

"Word is you were threatening her this evening?"

"Whose word?"

I smoked.

"You get that from Al?"

I watched the smoke waft into the air.

"I bet that's not all you'd like to get from her."

I stared at The Rat's beady eyes. Took another slow smoke. Then said, "Tell me about Charlie."

"She serves drinks and what this place alleges is food. Doesn't like it much if you grab her," he said with a wink.

"You do that a lot?" I asked.

"No."

"Did you grab her earlier?"

The Rat swallowed.

"Why'd you threaten her?"

"I didn't *threaten* her."

"Then what did you do?"

The Rat cleared his throat. "I reminded her of some things."

"What things?"

"Charlie owes me some money. A sizeable amount."

"Why?"

"She backed the wrong side. Repeatedly."

"Gambling?"

The Rat nodded.

"Charlie's into you?"

"That's right."

"For how much?"

The Rat looked down at his hand, then extended two fingers to the side.

"Two hundred dollars?" I asked.

He laughed. "Two thousand."

I couldn't hide the surprise and took a drag on the cigarette. I did some math. Not the kind that would compute how many ball games or fights or horse races it would take to rack up two grand in gambling debts, nor how long it would take a girl like Charlie to make that amount of money. No, the math I did was more like connecting dots. Charlie owed The Rat money. Daisy's safe was empty. She'd been tracking Charlie's hours. The dots connected, but not in a way that made sense.

"You know, if you're serious about solving this murder, you ought to talk to Peaches."

"Yeah, why's that?"

The Rat leaned forward, and dropped his voice. He hadn't been talking loudly to begin with. "Did you know Peaches wants to buy this place?"

"I know."

"Daisy said no."

"You think Peaches killed her?"

"It's a theory. Better than whatever you're sniffing at, that I killed Daisy because Charlie owed me money? Seriously, you're a detective?"

I let the remark go with another hit on the cigarette. I might be headed back to Al for another Johnny Walker Black too.

"Besides," The Rat said, sitting back and straightening his shirt cuff, "I told you earlier, the boys and I were here for the entire performance."

"Yeah, you told me."

"Peaches wasn't."

I pretended not to be interested. Not too interested. "No?"

"No. Just as Lizzie broke into her closing number, Peaches got up and left."

"Left where?"

"You'll have to ask her."

"I mean what door? She go outside? She go powder her nose? Make a phone call?"

The Rat pointed, and followed the point with a turn of his head, toward the alcove off the bar, an alcove that contained both the men's room and the ladies' room, a pay phone, and a back staircase to the second level.

I smoked.

"Now come on, Detective, when can we get out of here?"

"Got some kneecaps to break, maybe somebody to fit for cement shoes?"

"So colorful."

I took one last drag on the cigarette, then flipped it at Tony-Boy. "You can leave when I say so," I said, then stood and went to get more Scotch from Al.

eight

CHARLIE'S GAMBLING DEBTS had nothing to do with Daisy's murder, but I decided to talk to her before Peaches for a couple of reasons. One is I wanted Peaches to wait as long as possible, make her antsy, maybe make her slip up. Two, I'm scared of her, and was stalling. So I took the bottle from Al with a promise to pay off that tab soon, cradled two tumblers in my hand, and caught Charlie's attention. I nodded toward an empty table away from listening ears, and we sat down on opposite sides of it.

Charlie has long blond hair that she keeps in a ponytail, which is usually stretched straight out as it follows her around. Cute if not beautiful, she's young and always smiling, somehow. I don't envy her, delivering booze to a bunch of bums and slapping away their hands, trying to take food orders and deliver plates while not getting in the way of an audience, hustling all the time. I've never seen her not hustling. She ought to be called Charlie Hustle.

"Something on your mind?" Charlie asked.

I shook off whatever it was and poured the Scotch. I slid one tumbler to her.

"Thanks," she said.

"I have to ask the questions, Charlie."

"I know."

"Daisy worked you hard, it's no secret."

"She worked everybody hard. Worked me so hard I didn't have a spare minute during Lizzie's performance. I couldn't have killed Daisy if I wanted to--and I didn't."

I took a drink. So did she.

"Al said you got into it with The Rat," I said. We were far enough away from people, and Gramps was tinkering at the piano, so it was a private conversation.

Charlie played with her tumbler, tracing the rim. "I owe him money."

I took another sip and waited.

She played with the tumbler some more, tipping it, rotating it, dang near spilling a finger of Johnny Walker Black. "Almost two thousand. He wanted it back."

"How'd you get into The Rat for that kind of money?"

She stopped fiddling with the tumbler and looked up. "Baseball. I'm a sucker for the Tigers. They couldn't beat their way out of a paper sack, but . . . I keep betting on them."

"With The Rat?"

She offered a sheepish smile.

I took another sip.

"I told him I didn't have it yet, but would soon."

"Like from Daisy's safe?"

"In a manner of speaking."

I frowned.

"Daisy was letting me work extra hours to make up the debt. I've been spending every waking minute here, doing anything and everything--cleaning, changing grease traps in the kitchen, doing Daisy's laundry, running various errands. I almost had half, to pay back The Rat and get him off my back. Now . . ." She drained the tumbler and clunked it down. "Why would I kill the person paying me the money I needed?"

"You wouldn't, Charlie."

"You know who else wouldn't?"

"Who?"

"Moose."

I nodded. "Why are you telling me that?"

She bit her lip and it was, like I said before, cute. "Because I saw him arguing with Daisy a few days ago. Moose doesn't usually argue with anybody, so it stuck out." She leaned forward. "But he wouldn't do it, TJ."

"I know, Charlie. I know."

"So who did?"

I lifted my tumbler, took a drink, and turned my eyes across the dining room to where a knockout sat impatiently by herself. I set down the tumbler and sighed. There was no putting it off any longer.

nine

PEACHES HAS NO business frequenting the Palisades Club. She is way out of its league. The Palisades Club is for regular people, nine-to-fivers. I've never heard where Peaches works, if she does at all, and she is anything but regular.

For one thing, she's six-feet tall, so she looks most men in their eye if not their bald spot. For another, she's stunningly beautiful. I mean head-turning gorgeous. She augments her beauty with top-of-the-line clothing, jewelry, and accessories (I've never seen her carry the same purse). And don't get me started on her long, golden hair, which is magnificent in its own right.

Tonight, she wore a teal V-neck dress, a furry stole, and silver bangles that clanged whenever she moved her arm, which was often, judging by the empties on her table. But she was sober as a judge--her sapphire eyes told me that as I approached, pulled out a chair, and sat down.

"Hello, Peaches."

"Tommy," she purred with disdain. I hated it when she called me Tommy. Grown men don't go by the name Tommy. Thomas or Tom or TJ--heck, "You" would work fine. I swallowed and reached into my pocket, pulled out and unwrapped a sucker, and crunched on it. I spent a moment pondering the sucker--I couldn't remember where it had come from or why I was sucking on it now, but somehow it seemed important. I shrugged it off and looked at Peaches, my eyes now resting on a sparkling silver pendant around her neck, visible because the stole was unwrapped.

"You didn't come over here just to make this sterling conversation, did you?"

I crunched on the sucker again. "I think you killed Daisy," I said.

Peaches laughed. "Why would I kill Daisy?"

Noting that wasn't a denial, I said, "Because you wanted her club."

"This dive?"

"If it's such a dive, why do you spend so much time here?"

She leveled her eyes at me, and they nearly made two holes. "You're slobbering," she finally said.

I took one last hard lick and yanked the sucker out of my mouth. I set it on a napkin, an action that seemed to displease Peaches and thus pleased me. "You haven't answered the question."

She exhaled an icy breath. "So I wanted the club. That doesn't make me a killer."

"Did you send her a bunch of dead daises?"

Peaches frowned.

"'You get what you deserve,'" I said from memory. "Signed, '-P' as in Peaches."

"That still doesn't make me a killer."

"So it was you?"

"I wanted the club. It has good bones," she said, gesturing around with her long fingers. "She wouldn't sell, and I was mad. So yeah, I sent her some flowers. *They* were what she deserved, not murder." She shook her head. "I didn't kill her."

"Where were you when she was killed?"

"How would I know when she was killed?"

"During Lizzie's last number. She hit the high note and somebody pulled the trigger."

"Well, it wasn't me."

"The Rat saw you leave just about that time."

"The Rat's a rat. And he smells bad."

"I don't disagree. Where were you?"

She lifted a loose strand of hair off her brow with her finger. Then she bored her eyes into me again. "With Sherm."

"Sherm. Sherman? Officer Sherman?"

She lifted her chin a fraction.

"What were you doing with Officer Sherman?"

"You're a grown-up, Tommy . . . sort of. Do the math."

I frowned, but hard. "You and Sherman are an item?"

Peaches raised her eyebrows.

"Convenient," I said. "But you could have hired somebody to do it. You've got plenty of money."

"I didn't. And you'll never be able to prove otherwise."

"That a challenge?"

"That's a fact."

I sat back. Was she playing games for games' sake, or to throw me off?

"Sherm will vouch for me, and my character."

"I hope you aren't playing games with him."

"I don't play games, Tommy." She leaned forward and winked. "But if I did, I would surely win."

I wasn't getting anywhere. No surprise.

Peaches took a sip of some clear liquid in her glass. "Besides, Daisy told me she had willed the club to Gramps over there," she said, gesturing with the glass at the piano.

"And if there's one person in the world who wouldn't sell it to me, it's him. Daisy's death doesn't help me one bit."

"Why wouldn't Gramps sell to you?"

"He hates me."

"Why's that?"

She shrugged. "You'll have to ask him." She drained the glass and set it down with a soft thud. "Else talk to Lizzie. It's no secret Daisy treated her horridly, and now that Daisy's gone, well . . ."

"Lizzie has an alibi."

"So do I. And a character witness. So why don't you go play *your* games somewhere else."

I sighed, but had nothing else to counter with. So I pushed back from the table.

"Oh, and take *your* lollipop with you, would you, Tommy?"

ten

GRAMPS WAS STILL tinking away at the

piano as I wandered back over to the stage. He looked up at me without slowing down. The song was familiar, but I couldn't place it at the moment. But that didn't matter.

"More questions?" Gramps asked.

"A couple," I said, turning to look back at the dining room. Nobody had moved--The Rat, Peaches, Al behind the bar, Charlie at the table where we'd talked, the other couples. Sherman and O'Brien still stood by the front entrance, a subtle reminder. Moose was in the shadows offstage. I turned to Gramps.

"Is it true that Daisy willed the place to you?"

He looked at me and smiled, then nodded. He kept playing.

"So you now own the Palisades Club?"

"Well, once it works its way through the legal system I suppose I will."

"Why you, Gramps?"

He finished out a few notes, then lowered his hands and slowly turned on the piano bench to face me. "I told you that Daisy and I go way back. Truth is, I knew her father. I won't bore you with all the details, but I owed him from a long time ago. So," he said with a slow scratch of his jaw, "I promised to look after his daughter after he died. Heart attack, a number of years back. Big one, then a little one that killed him about a week after that."

"What do you mean by 'look after' Daisy?"

Gramps shrugged. "We never really specified. But that's why I play here every night, so I can be around, keep close." He leaned forward. "I've met quite a few people over the years, in the industry, so I've been able to help her make some talent connections, some agents. And I've lent her money a few times, when business was struggling. Charlie and Al too, when they hit some tough spots." He smiled. "My daddy used to quote the Good Book, '*Freely ye have received, freely give.*'"

"You've received freely?"

"Granddad made big money working for the railroad. I've never *had* to work a day in my life, but what kind of life would that be for a man? And like I said, it helped me keep an eye on Daisy." He looked down. "Not close enough, though, I guess."

I put a hand on his shoulder. "There was nothing you could have done."

He nodded, maybe convinced, maybe not.

"What are you going to do with the place?"

"Haven't thought much about it. Never expected to have to. Figured I'd go long before Daisy."

"Gonna sell it?" I asked.

"Might. To the right person."

"Peaches?"

"No way."

"Why not?"

He looked down. "I'd rather not talk about it."

"It'd sure help me if you did."

Gramps swallowed hard. Then he swiveled back and began playing a song, a familiar one again, but one I couldn't place. It was sad, and yet beautiful, and for some reason made me think of the ocean.

"Back before the war," he said in a quiet, husky voice, "Peaches and my grandson were an item. He was handsome, and she's, well, Peaches, and they fell hard and fast," he said, then ran off a couple measures or bars or whatever. "Before he went over to fight the Krauts, they were pledged to be married. They were passionately in love, Mr. James."

I nodded, then waited as he played some more of that song at which I didn't know whether to frown or smile.

"My grandson got hurt by a grenade, fragments in his leg, his side, and his face. Crippled him. He'll walk with a limp for the rest of his life. Also has scarring on the left side of his face. Although not major, it's noticeable." He lifted his hands and looked up. "When he came home, Peaches would have nothing to do with him. He was no longer a perfect specimen, and she turned her back on him."

"That's cold," I said, squinting out toward where she sat haughtily in that teal V-neck dress.

"The Good Book says to '*forgive our debtors,*' but I can't bring myself to forgive her for what she did to him." He shook his head. "I wouldn't sell her a cup of cold water if she were dying of thirst."

"I don't blame you, Gramps."

"Anything else you need from me?"

My eyes had settled on Sherman across the room. Something didn't add up, him and Peaches.

"Mr. James?"

I turned back to Gramps. "No. No, that's all. Thanks again, Gramps."

It was time to check my math.

eleven

OFFICER SHERMAN AND I found privacy outside, under the awning over the front door of the Palisades Club. The rain was pitter-pattering, soft little tat-a-tat-tat-tats on the awning's fabric. I lit a cigarette and turned to Sherman.

"What's this about, TJ?"

I took a drag and exhaled. "First, I need your promise that this is confidential, just between you and me."

"Of course."

"I mean it, Sherman. You can't tell your buddies, your fellow cops, your girlfriend."

"My girlfriend," he said, blushing.

"Handsome guy like you has to draw attention from the ladies, right?"

He blushed some more.

"Promise me, Sherman."

"I promise, TJ."

I nodded and took a hit of nicotine. I blew it out and dropped my bomb. "How long have you and Peaches been seeing each other?"

Sherman nearly swallowed his tongue.

"You're her alibi, 'Sherm,' so don't leave her hanging."

"We, uh . . . I mean, it's--um--it's been a . . . a few months."

"Serious?"

"I don't . . . I don't know yet. I mean, it is for me, but . . ."

"Were you two together during the closing song?"

He nodded.

"That's why you were right across the street when Moose found you?"

Another nod.

I shook my head. "How and why, Sherman?"

"How and why what?"

"How did you get a girl that looks like Peaches, who has Peaches' money, who runs in Peaches' circle, to fall for a beat cop like you? And why would a stand-up guy like you fall for a girl like her?"

"That's not fair, TJ." He shook his head. "Peaches is a . . ."

"She's what, Sherman?"

"She's not just a beautiful woman. She's a beautiful soul. I know she rubs some people the wrong way, but deep down . . . she's amazing, TJ."

I inhaled on the cigarette again.

"I'm telling you, TJ, not only could Peaches not have done it because we were together, but she wouldn't have done it. It's just not in her."

I sighed.

"You don't believe me?"

"No, I do believe you. Just be careful, Sherman."

"Careful?"

"I wouldn't want to see a nice guy like you get hurt."

He frowned.

I smoked.

The rain kept tat-a-tat-tat-tatting.

"Are you making headway?" he asked finally.

"I don't know. I need to think a minute."

"Alone?"

"Yeah," I said. I flicked the butt of my cigarette into the gutter, then reached for another. "Get everybody together in there," I said. "Have Al set 'em up with drinks or whatever. I'll be in in a few minutes."

"All together? You going to reveal the murderer?"

"Just get 'em together," I said, "everybody who's down there."

"Okay, you got it, TJ."

He left, and I lit my cigarette. I listened to the rain some more. And I thought, long and hard.

twelve

*A*FTER *MAYBE TEN* minutes, I was
getting cold. So I flicked my latest butt into
the street and headed inside. Sherman and
O'Brien had assembled everyone at a few of
the tables near the front, by the stage.
Gramps still sat at the piano, but silently
now. Moose leaned against a support column
off the front of the stage. Al and Charlie had
both stopped working, for once, and sat at a
table with Peaches--a different table than
the one she'd been at before. The Rat and the
meatheads had moved too, as had several

other patrons, including the duo at the bar. I scanned my eyes over the group, and then met Lizzie's for just a second as she stood back in the shadows, still magnificent in that red dress.

They all looked intently at me, and I took advantage of the attention by slowly lighting one last cigarette. I took a breath, exhaled, and looked at them again. "One of you shot Daisy," I said evenly. A few people shifted in their seats. Peaches sighed audibly.

"All of you had a motive," I said. "Lizzie and Gramps were on stage when she was killed, so they couldn't have done it."

No one argued with me, and I took a drag on the cigarette.

"I don't think Moose would hurt Daisy."

"I wouldn't, Mr. James," he said.

"But you did argue with her the other day."

He looked as if *I'd* shot *him*.

"Why?" I asked gently.

"She was . . . Sh-sh-she . . ."

"Take your time, Moose."

He nodded. "She wasn't treatin' Miss Lizzie right, Mr. James. She'd . . ." He looked toward Lizzie. "She hit her. I told Miss Daisy that wasn't right."

"What'd she say?"

"She made some excuse, said it was complicated." He shook his head. "I didn't really understand what she meant, Mr. James. It still seemed wrong to me."

I nodded. I smoked.

"Who says it has to be one of us?" Peaches asked.

"Who else?" I asked.

"Anybody off the street. This isn't exactly the best neighborhood."

"Door wasn't jimmied. Had to be somebody with a key or somebody already inside, and all those people are here."

"If one of us shot her, where's the gun, Detective?" The Rat asked.

"Lots of places to hide a gun," I said.

"And these two bloodhounds didn't find it?" he asked, jerking a thumb at Sherman and O'Brien.

"Not yet," I said.

He pressed down his vest, then stood. "I think you've got nothing, Detective."

"I've got you as a part-owner of the club who wanted it all, who'd tried to lure Daisy's talent away, who got a crack in the head for his efforts. And more than enough reputation to be guilty by."

"Except I was sitting here when she was killed, and you checked my gun. You've got nothing."

I took a drag on the cigarette.

"Now, my associates here and I have been good sports. But unless you plan to arrest us, we've had enough. We're leaving."

Johnny-Boy and Tony-Boy both stood. I stared at them and smoked some more. "I'm not having you arrested," I said. "Not yet."

With defiant glares, all three of them marched past me. I turned and watched them, catching a glance from Sherman, wondering what he should do. I shook my head and let them go. When the door closed, I turned back to the group.

"Does that mean it was one of us?" Charlie asked.

"You had opportunity," I said. "The way you hustle around, in and out of the kitchen, nobody would have noticed you being gone for a few minutes." I shook my head. "But you don't have a motive, not with Daisy letting you work extra hours to pay off your debts."

She looked down.

"Al, meanwhile, smokes the same cigarettes found in Daisy's office. But I doubt she's that clumsy to leave one behind. And she never leaves the bar."

"Does that mean we can go?" Al asked.

I nodded toward the door.

She winked at me and Charlie offered a half smile as they both got up and walked to the door. I focused on Peaches.

"Oh please, Tommy."

"You admitted to sending Daisy the dead flowers and note, and you'd kill in a second if it'd help you out. But Daisy's death all but guarantees you'll never get your hands on the Palisades Club, and that's the only reason I'm letting you out of here."

"That, and you wouldn't dare cross me." Her eyes boring into me, she stood, drained her glass, and flipped her stole around her neck. Still staring at me, she sauntered toward the door.

"Who's left, Mr. James?" Moose asked.

"Nobody," I said with disdain. I looked at the rest of the patrons, all strangers. "You're all free to go."

They wasted no time getting up and hurrying out. Gramps shuffled down after them. "Give it a night's rest," he said, patting me on the shoulder. "Maybe it will make sense then."

"Yeah, maybe."

Sherman shuffled over. "You're really giving up?"

I shrugged. "There's nothing to prove anyone did it, even though one of them had to. But no, I'm not giving up. There's just nothing more I can do tonight."

"Okay. You want anything more from us?"

"No. You've done plenty. Thanks, Sherman," I said, shaking his hand. "O'Brien."

He too shook my hand.

"We'll see someone comes and gets the body first thing in the morning," Sherman said.

I nodded as they turned to go. I looked to Moose, who stood in front of me. He swallowed. "We have to get him, Mr. James. Daisy's killer can't just get off."

"He won't, Moose." I nodded toward the door. "You head on home. I'll lock up."

"Yes, sir, Mr. James."

He followed the two officers out of the building, and I took a long drag on the cigarette. I pulled out a chair at the nearest table and sat back, thinking over the last hour or so. Replaying questions asked and questions left unasked, answers given, possibilities missed or clues unexplored. With a sigh, I tipped my hat up, thinking I couldn't have done anything more . . . except maybe have Al pour me another drink before she left.

I puffed on the cigarette and turned my head toward a series of rhythmic clicks, interspersed with soft swooshes. From out of the shadows, Lizzie slowly strode toward me. She stopped just in front of me, looking like a million bucks.

"What will happen now?" she asked.

"The cops will sniff around a little more, probably turn the place inside out looking for a gun. Eventually, they'll conclude it was a random robbery--someone sneaked up from the inside, maybe through the window. Maybe," I said, reaching into my pocket, "they'll even guess that somebody stole a key off Al, Charlie, Gramps . . . or you," I said, holding up a brass key on a small leather strap.

Lizzie looked at me, then at the key.

"In a few weeks, they'll forget all about it, and then . . ." I extended the key to her.

Her eyes narrowed as she took the key, squeezing it in a gloved hand for a moment. "A few weeks."

"We've waited this long. What's a few more weeks?"

"Eternity," she said, then broke into a wide smile as she tossed the key onto the table. She took a few steps in her stilettos, stopped beside me, then sat on my lap. She made a show of pulling off her silver gloves, draping them on the table beside the key. Then she tipped my fedora back and wrapped her arms around my neck. "How'd I do?"

"Brilliantly."

"'You will catch whoever did this, won't you?' That wasn't too much?"

"It was perfect."

"Everything go as planned?"

I nodded. "Well, almost. Who knew the Rat would switch cigarette brands after I put a butt of his brand in her ashtray? But yeah, otherwise, it went off without a hitch."

"You get the cash in the safe?"

"Only a few grand, but it'll buy us tickets out of here."

"A few weeks?"

"At the most."

Her cheeks practically squeaked as she smiled. Then the smile slowly faded. "Did you . . . did you feel any remorse when you pulled the trigger?"

I very gently traced my fingertip around the bruise on her face. "Not one bit."

She took hold of my hand and held it by her cheek.

I looked up into her baby blues. "She'll never hurt you again, angel."

"I know," she said, fighting off tears. She moved her hands to clutch my face in them. "Thank you, Thomas."

Lizzie kissed me then, and I kissed her back, long, slow, and sweet.

thirteen

*O*UR *KISSING WENT* on for quite a while.

Eventually, Lizzie wrapped her arms around me again, then moved her hands to my shoulders and . . . She started shaking me.

Only it wasn't Lizzie anymore. It was . . . Daisy? Then it wasn't Daisy but . . .

"Maggie?"

"Jack, what's going on?"

Jackson blinked a few times. He was not sitting on a chair at the Palisades Club but laying in his king bed. And his wife was leaning over him. He inched himself onto his elbows, and Maggie pushed herself upright, one hand going to her lower back. "You were making a weird noise, like you were slurping soup."

He turned to look at the red numbers of the clock beside the bed. 4:10.

"Slurping?" he managed.

"Or sucking."

"I was . . . I . . ." He felt his tongue in his gunky mouth. "I need coffee." He started to push out of bed.

"Jack, it's the middle of the night."

"We need to get used to it, right?"

He trudged downstairs to the kitchen, quickly set a small pot of coffee to brewing, and stepped out onto the deck to get some fresh air. It was cool, and he was barefoot in pajama bottoms and a T-shirt, but he didn't care.

None of it was real. Not the club, not a dead owner, not a flirty bartender or sleazy mobster or . . . Lizzie making out on his lap. Lizzie . . . Elizabeth . . .

The door opened and Maggie stepped out, now in a flannel shirt and jeans to go with her slippers. She held a mug of coffee in both hands, then extended it to him. "Another dream?" she asked as he took a long gulp, never mind the scalding heat.

"Yeah."

"Hayes?" she asked, leaning against the deck railing.

"No. Worse."

"Stan Kroenke threatening to relocate the Rams again?"

"Don't even joke about that," he said, taking another gulp.

"Well, we're both up now, and my hands are freezing. Want to tell me about it?"

"I was a private eye," Jackson said.

"Sounds familiar."

He shook his head. "I was back in the forties though, trench coat and fedora, smoking like a fiend, and I was investigating a murder at this little jazz club--the Palisades Club--and . . . I was also the murderer."

"Intriguing. You should write a short story."

"You were the victim, Maggie."

"Me?"

"Well, the old broad who owned the club, named Daisy."

"I was an old broad named Daisy?"

He nodded and took a drink.

"What makes you think it was me?"

"Because I killed you to run off with Sam."

"Sam?"

"'Lizzie,' short for Elizabeth. Her middle name."

"I warned you about that extra chalupa."

"Maggie, it was weird. She was this sweet but sexy jazz singer, with long gloves, and Grandpa was her piano player, quoting Scripture at me. The bouncer was this big black guy named Moose, and don't tell Reggie, but Moose was a little slow. And Mouse was a gangster called The Rat, with two goons who never spoke, like Darryl and Darryl on *Newhart*, and . . ."

"What?"

"Ashley was the waitress, Charlie, who loved the Tigers."

"Charlie?"

"Charlie Hustle, Pete Rose, a baseball player, and Ashley was in police softball leagues."

She raised an eyebrow.

"Hey, I dreamt it, not made it up."

"Your brain still made it up. Didn't Pete Rose play for the Reds?"

"Yes, but Magnum loved the Tigers."

"What's Magnum have to do with anything?"

"My name was Thomas James."

"Magnum and Rockford."

"Uh-huh. And . . . Aha, that's why I was looking at her tie."

"What?"

"The bartender was a girl named Al, who called me by my last name and served me Johnnie *Walker* Black, and wore a silver and black tie. Walker was a Raiders fan, and when we were undercover all those years ago she went by the name Allie." He took a drink. "Oh, and Peaches."

"Peaches?"

"This blond bombshell with an attitude."

"Hillary?"

"Who was sweet on a beat cop named Sherman."

Maggie shook her head.

"Grant's middle name is Sherman."

"Maybe it was more than chalupas."

"Right? This is scary."

"It's not scary, Jack," she said, coming over to stand beside him. "It's weird, even for you, I'll admit, but that's it."

"I don't know. I haven't dreamt about Sam in ages, since we got married, and I thought . . . Especially now."

She placed a hand on his arm. "Jack, it's a dream. I'm not worried."

"Okay."

She reached up and kissed his cheek. "But I am tired. You coming back to bed?"

"I don't think I'll ever sleep again."

"Maybe in your next dream I'll come back to life as a hot zombie and we'll get revenge on 'Lizzie' together."

"I think I need to start seeing Zachary again. I wonder if he does remotes."

She kissed him again, this time on the lips. "I'll see you in the morning."

"I think I'll watch the sunrise and ponder sleep habits."

"Okay. Just promise me you won't obsess over this. It was just a dream."

"If you promise you'll come visit me in the psych ward," he said lifting his mug again.

"Deal."

"And you," he said, stepping forward and placing his hand on Maggie's stomach, "promise me you'll take after your mommy and not your daddy."